Shot of Chaos

Roberto Brecht

D1738679

Roberto Brecht

First edition, 2025
ISBN 979-8-3161-0837-4

Preface

Shot of Chaos is a collection of short stories where the real and the imaginary blur together, and chaos reigns supreme.

With tales that bring terror in its various forms, the chaotic and the unexpected are served in short, impactful doses. Horrible monsters, unscrupulous killers, vengeful spirits (or not), and the worst of all horrors—your own mind—await you in the pages to come.

Get ready to indulge in the Shot of Chaos.

Roberto Brecht

Shot of Chaos

Roberto Brecht

Teddy Bear

The longing was so strong that she went to bed crying. For a long time, she thought she wouldn't be able to fall asleep, but after so many days of sadness, she finally found some rest. Unfortunately, the rest didn't last long. It was in the middle of the night when she was startled awake by the sound of a child crying. Tears came again, but she soon recognized her daughter's voice and got up. She was tired, but she couldn't abandon her daughter now. The pain she felt was great, but it was nothing compared to the pain of her little girl who had lost her father.

As she entered her daughter's room, she noticed that her daughter was pretending to sleep, hugging a teddy bear that she and her husband had given her when she was still a baby. Her daughter could have fooled her if it weren't for the sobs she couldn't control. She lay down next to the girl, and they cried together for a few minutes. Soon after, her daughter looked into her eyes and asked why this had happened. She had hoped she would never have to explain life and death to anyone, let alone to her daughter who had just begun her life.

Taking a deep breath, she composed herself and explained that things happen without explanation, but it was necessary to move on and turn longing into memories. She explained that one day the pain would pass, and only the best of those who had gone would remain. Her daughter nodded as if she understood. But she started crying again shortly after. Not usually one to do this, she picked her daughter up and took her to her own bed. They both needed it. They would sleep together, and tomorrow everything would be better.

Once in bed, she hugged her daughter, and her daughter hugged the teddy bear even tighter. Automatically, she began to stroke the child's hair, and slowly, the girl stopped crying. A wave of sadness washed over her again as she realized she missed the smell of her daughter's hair. Her eyes grew heavy, and she felt she was about to fall asleep again when she heard her daughter's voice from afar. She said she wasn't sad about her father, but rather for seeing her mother so sad.

She woke up alone in bed, hugging her daughter's teddy bear. She felt as bad as she had every morning since the accident that took her family away, but her heart felt lighter. She needed to move on with her life. She got up, took a shower, and went to work, not remembering that the teddy bear was the last thing she had placed in her daughter's coffin before burying her.

Roberto Brecht

Wake

Despite hating wakes, she knew she couldn't miss this one.

She arrived quietly on that rainy day and entered the cemetery discreetly. As soon as she saw the deceased's family, she realized she didn't belong there.

Her relationship with the deceased had never been close. They knew each other, yes, but she had no idea who his friends were, his family, or the people close to him—none of that.

She decided to walk around the place and observe, trying to figure out exactly how to act. Contrary to what she had imagined, some people were laughing and having fun in a rather disrespectful way. There were also those who cried and those who were desperate, but they were in the minority. Overall, people remained quiet, and that's how she stayed.

After a closer look, she noticed that no one was truly silent. In low whispers, everyone was talking to each other. More than that, except for the family, no one seemed to care much about the deceased.

Some time later, the rain let up, and with it, the wake ended. The burial was approaching, and along with the coffin being carried to its final resting place, came the family, who were genuinely sad.

Two children and a wife. The entire ceremony was for them, the only ones who mattered.

Looking at them brought a painful lump to her throat. She had never seen them before, but witnessing their suffering created an instant empathy. She closed her eyes and focused; she was there for work and needed to be strong.

The coffin was lowered, the children hugged their mother, and the three of them wept profusely. Now, she couldn't look away from them.

This was why she hated funerals. She didn't need this empathy; it would only get in the way. Still, she fixed her gaze on the grieving family and stored that image in her memory.

She had a duty to fulfill. The contract she signed stated that the entire family had to die that night.

It would be easy. She just needed to wait for the ceremony to end, follow them, and finish them off the same way she had done with the man being buried.

She returned to her car and waited. She prepared her gun and followed the family's car, knowing that for the first time, she would cry during a job.

Roberto Brecht

Bridge

"I'm going crazy..." – That was his first thought upon seeing the man who disappeared into thin air in the middle of the street. So many people around, and yet again, he seemed to be the only one who noticed. He kept walking; he couldn't stop like last time, or people would start to notice, and the only thing he prided himself on was his sanity.

A few meters ahead was the office where he worked. He hurried inside, head down, not wanting to talk to anyone—just go to his room and forget what he had just seen.

Minutes passed, and he remained seated in his chair, not working, thinking about what could be happening. He didn't believe in God or anything that couldn't be proven, so not for a second did he consider that the disappearing people or the noises he heard could have any explanation other than his mind playing tricks on him. He decided to schedule a psychologist appointment that same day. He started working, and like the man that morning, the worry disappeared.

The next day, on his way to work, he remembered what had happened the day before, and along with that memory, he recalled that he should see a psychologist soon. But it wasn't the right time yet. He couldn't waste time on that; it wasn't a big deal. His work was at a crucial moment, his wife pregnant with their second child. It really wasn't the time.

He was working when he noticed it was already 9 PM. Another late day, and there was still so much to do. He decided to stay until 11:30 PM at the latest when his phone rang:

"Love, are you on your way? I know we agreed on 9:15, but I'll still need about 15 minutes to get ready, is that okay?"

It was their wedding anniversary. He couldn't cancel last minute again like the past two years. She had understood before, but he had promised it wouldn't happen again. Besides, it had been a long time since he had given her any attention.

"Okay, I'll be a little late, but I'll be there in time to pick you up."

"Work again?" she asked with a conclusive tone.

"Yes, but it won't stop me this time." He hung up the phone, turned off the computer, and left.

"You actually left!" she said as they drove off. It was the first time in three years that he had chosen her over work.

"I miss you two. Even more now that you're pregnant."

"Don't worry about me, I'm early in the pregnancy, and I know you'll be there when I need you. I'm more worried about our daughter; you barely see each other."

"I worry about her too. I hate coming home and finding her asleep every time. But it won't always be like this—just three more months of chaos until the bridge is finished, and then I'll be all yours."

"I hope so."

He hoped so too, but he knew that finishing the bridge would only be the beginning. If everything went well, he would revolutionize not only his field but also bring about real change in the world, and that would mean even more work. If it failed, he would be bankrupt, and that wasn't an option.

The reservation was at a fancy restaurant. They arrived right on time, and everything was perfect, except for the fact that he could only think about his work.

"Hello? Are you there?"

"Sorry. I was..."

"You always are. But try to forget about it for one night, for me."

"I will. Should I order more wine? Would you like some?"

"I'd love a little, can I have a sip of yours?"

"I already finished my glass."

"No, you didn't."

"It was empty just now, how can it..." That's when he realized it had happened again. Again, something small, but it was the frequency of these small things that was starting to scare him.

"Work again?" his wife said after a few seconds of silence.

"Uh... yes, I'm sorry."

The rest of the dinner was like the dinners they usually had at home. He was silent, tense, with a distant look of someone deep in thought, and she tried to keep the conversation going, giving up after a few attempts.

As soon as they got home, she went straight to the bedroom and lay down on the bed without even taking off her clothes. He approached her, and she said, her voice unable to hide the tears:

"Three months. I can't take more than that."

He thought about hugging her but thought it might only make things worse. He had promised three months; he wished he could spend more time with her, but he knew it probably wouldn't happen, and worse, he hoped it wouldn't. He wanted success and was willing to pay the price for it.

He decided to go see his daughter; it had been so long since he had talked to her. Even if she was already asleep, it would be good to be with her.

Roberto Brecht

He entered the dark room quietly and sat on the bed. She was lying with her eyes closed. He kissed her cheek, and she opened her eyes, saying with the heavy breath of someone scared:

"Dad... can you see who's under my bed?"

"Sweetie, it's nothing, don't worry. I'm here."

"Dad..." she said again, her voice low, almost disappearing. "You need to see... please."

He was tired, but it had been so long since he had talked to his daughter that he thought he should do this to calm her down. He got out of bed, knelt, and looked.

At first, there was nothing to see, but then he noticed movement in the dark. He squinted and saw what looked like hair. It was hair. Someone's hair.

A chill ran down his spine, starting at the base and rising to the top before returning. He was paralyzed when he realized the hair was moving; the hidden face was rising. It was someone; there was really someone under the bed.

He passed out.

The alarm clock rang. 5:30 AM, time to wake up. He was in his bed with his wife beside him. He began to stretch when he remembered the previous night and got up at once. His wife stirred in bed but didn't wake up.

Shot of Chaos

He stood still for a few seconds. "What happened?" he thought. He remembered the dinner, the wine, coming home... his daughter. "It was a dream. It had to be... So why am I standing here, afraid?"

Step by step, he went to his daughter's room; the door was slightly open. He decided to enter but turned on the light first.

His daughter was sleeping in bed normally, but that didn't calm him. He needed to kneel and look, but just thinking about it made the chill return. Slowly, he began to kneel, and with every inch closer to the floor, his hair stood on end. His mind told him he should do it, but his body was on alert and seemed to refuse.

Finally, his mind won, and before he knew it, his knees were on the floor. Then he looked. There was nothing under the bed. But the feeling that something was wrong didn't leave him. He stood up and quickly left the room without looking at the bed, afraid of what he might find.

He arrived at work about an hour later. He sat at his desk and once again forgot everything that had happened.

It was 11 PM. He was still at the office. His body was tired; he had given his all over the past three years, but the last few months had been more than he thought he could endure.

He turned off the computer and stretched in his chair. He had made incredible progress on the bridge and was increasingly sure it would surprise the world. News had already started to spread in the media, it was only a matter of time before it was finally inaugurated. A new concept of a bridge, where every detail mattered, a project he had dedicated more than three years of work to—a dream that had lasted his entire life and was now about to come true.

He stood up and opened his office door. The office was empty, as usual when he left. He walked to the exit when he noticed movement beside him. He looked and saw one of the chairs spinning.

He stopped the chair with his hand. He closed his eyes and took a deep breath. He knew he shouldn't open his eyes. He knew what would happen the moment he opened them, but he didn't want to confirm it. He was so close, and now, of all times, his mind was failing him?!

He opened his eyes. In the chair he still held sat a man in a suit. He was looking down, hands on his knees, as if sad.

He knew that if the man in the suit raised his head and looked at him, it would be the end. He would have lost all his sanity. But the man kept his head down. He let go of the chair and took two steps back; the man remained seated, motionless.

He wanted to turn and run back to his office, but he couldn't turn, nor could he enter his office, afraid of what might happen when he opened the door.

Shot of Chaos

He had always been so rational, and now, facing what couldn't be understood, he didn't know what to do. Without thinking, he closed his eyes and kept them closed until he couldn't stand not knowing what was happening anymore. He opened his eyes, and the office was empty again.

He needed a psychologist. Urgently.

"How long have you been having these hallucinations?" asked the old man.

"I don't know. I think I've always had them, but I never realized they weren't real."

"And are you sure what you're seeing isn't real?"

"Until recently, I was sure it was real. That the person turned a corner when I wasn't looking, that the shadows were just impressions, that the noises were normal. In short, I trusted that my mind would never betray me. Now everything has changed, and I no longer know what's real or not."

"But how can you be sure? It's possible they're just coincidences, don't you think?"

"No, it's not a coincidence. I've always relied on rationality; the things I described can be explained, but some of the things I've seen don't make sense— they can't happen. Logic doesn't allow it. So, the only explanation I have is that my mind is doing this to me. And that can't happen, not now."

"If your mind is really doing this to you, how can you trust it to tell you what is and isn't rational? What is and isn't real?"

"What do you mean?"

"You said you know something isn't real because it's illogical. If a person appears or disappears into thin air, you conclude that it can't happen in the real world, so it doesn't exist and is a hallucination, right?"

"Yes, exactly."

"And what if your mind is creating more than the unreal? What if it's also creating illusions that resemble the real world?"

"That means... I could... What day is it today?"

"Tuesday, August 15."

"No, it can't be... The inauguration is today! I... I can't be here... I'm not here!"

The same chill he felt in his daughter's room ran through his entire body. His eyes were closed. He heard a loud, strange noise. He had the impression he was back in reality, but how could he be sure of anything?

He turned his head as if not wanting to see what was about to happen in front of him and opened his eyes. Clouds. He was on a plane. He didn't remember how he got there, only that this was where he was supposed to be. August 15, the day he had been waiting for. He would see his creation today; it would be the first day of the rest of his life.

He had a few hours left until the big moment, the first hours with no commitments in years. He tried to remember the last three months, but everything seemed blurry—just vague memories that didn't connect. His wife crying, his daughter in a car driving away, his empty bed. The empty office. No matter how hard he tried, he couldn't piece the information together.

He tried a little harder to remember, but then he realized he simply didn't care. It was his day. The day to see his bridge supporting a weight that had never been considered possible. Nothing else mattered today.

In all his life, time had never passed so slowly. The few hours left felt like days now that he had no commitments. He began to mentally review all the hypotheses and models that had been tested. In theory, there would be no errors, but he knew that a mistake in any detail would be the end.

That's when he realized he couldn't remember anything related to work from the last three months. He had worked; there was no doubt about that, but he didn't know on what. What if something had been forgotten? What if his bridge failed? What if he failed? How would he face the world? How would he face himself?

Roberto Brecht

He no longer trusted his mind. In fact, he no longer trusted anything, not even his bridge.

Despair took over. An internal struggle where he questioned what would happen. He had always imagined he could make mistakes, but he was sure it wasn't a possibility. However, now he couldn't think of anything else.

And then, the moment arrived. Before he knew it, he was in front of his bridge, with all the press, politicians, and important businessmen around him. He couldn't speak, only think that everything would go wrong. At that moment, he noticed something else he hadn't seen before. Neither his wife nor his daughter was with him. What had happened? How could he have skipped those three months and lost his family, sanity, and confidence?

He began to walk. Without noticing, he was crossing the bridge with a crowd behind him, believing this was the historic walk of a man who had dreamed of this moment his entire life.

He, however, just walked and ignored the crowd following him. The only thing he could notice was the silhouette of a person sitting on the bridge's railing, looking down.

As he walked, the silhouette became clearer, and he realized it was a man. Not just any man—it was the man in the suit from his office, in the same position as the first time he had seen him. He continued until he was close enough to recognize him. He had the same face he had seen throughout his life. His own face.

He stood beside him for a while, without fear this time. Slowly, the man in the suit raised his head until he looked directly at him. With sad eyes, he said:

"This is your big moment. How do you feel?"

"I don't know," he replied. "My moment has just begun." And he jumped off the bridge.

He opened his eyes, startled.

He was in his office; his wife had just called to say she would be a few minutes late. It was their wedding anniversary, and he couldn't be late this time.

He hung up the phone, turned off the computer, and left, in such a hurry that he didn't even notice the man in the suit who turned on his computer and started working in his place.

Roberto Brecht

Cabin

"Who's there?" – she asked while knocking on the cabin door after hearing the muffled scream coming from inside.

Nothing but more muffled screams. She kept knocking on the door, feeling the fear return. Because of this, she retraced her steps in her mind, trying to remember how she had ended up at the cabin in the middle of nowhere.

She remembered the trail with her friends, the argument they had, and her decision to go off alone. She also remembered the pain of waking up in the middle of the forest after slipping on a rock and realizing she was alone in the dark.

Since then, she had been walking, with no sign of her friends or the trail she was supposed to follow. She felt hunger, thirst, exhaustion, and, above all, fear.

However, the fear subsided when she saw the cabin standing alone in the middle of the forest. A brief hope emerged, only to vanish when she heard the muffled scream.

Shot of Chaos

She only stopped knocking when the screams grew louder and the icy sensation running up her spine began to paralyze her.

Before she became completely unable to act, she decided to walk around the cabin. The person inside surely knew where they were and could help her. She looked through the windows, but the darkness inside the cabin seemed even deeper than outside.

She tried to open the door, even though she was sure it would be locked. At the same time, she heard the screams from inside growing even more desperate.

She knew she wouldn't be welcome, but if the person inside was desperate, she was even more so. That's why she didn't think twice before breaking the cabin window.

The screams stopped. She found it strange, but she didn't care anymore. Even the fear was gone. All she could think about was not dying of hunger and escaping the darkness of that forest.

With difficulty, she climbed through the window and found herself in a new darkness. Finally, she would be saved. She just had to find the source of the screams and ask for help. But before she could start looking, she noticed that the air inside was heavy, as if the place had been dead for years.

She needed fresh air. She turned to breathe in the forest air, but there was no more forest, no more window. She was alone in the dark, trapped inside something she couldn't understand.

She screamed with all her might.

In response, she heard a knock and her own voice asking from outside, "Who's there?"

Christmas Lunch

"It's great to see all of you here today..." – Rute spoke awkwardly, looking at her children. She couldn't stop blaming herself for the family's pain and, even more, for the aggressive looks her husband gave her for insisting on having everyone together today.

"The food is good," said Raimundo, ignoring what his wife had said and shooting another angry glance in her direction as he took another sip of his beer. He hated these moments when he was forced to be with his children. Being with them reminded him that they were his responsibility, and that only made him angrier. That's why he kept planning to go to the bar later to drink the cachaça his friend had brought from Minas.

Lúcio remained quiet, as usual, when he was with his family. He could still remember the heat on his face from the slap his father had given him the last time he spoke his mind, and this was the first time in months he had returned to that house. At least this time, the food was good.

Grandma Antônia, on the other hand, wouldn't stop talking about how the food should have been prepared. She preferred to fill the sounds of the table herself rather than see her grandson disrespect her son again with his worldly behavior. She knew it was his wife's fault for never setting limits on the children, but she still hoped Jesus would save them.

Marta tried to exchange glances with Lúcio, but he wouldn't look up. He was the one in the family who had always understood her and would understand that she needed help. She knew that if she said something to everyone, the tears would only well up, and that would irritate her father again. She was already ready to kill herself and didn't need to suffer more by getting beaten before that.

"Mom, the food is really amazing! I can't stop thinking about dessert!" said Thiago, who, unlike his siblings, enjoyed every moment. Despite being, according to his father, the family's drug addict, he was the oldest and the most sensible.

He was the only one who knew this would be the last Christmas where he, his siblings, and his mother would suffer.

He was the only one who knew that with every sip of beer his father took, everything was getting closer to the end.

He was the only one who knew the poison would take effect that same day, probably at the bar where his father would spend his last Christmas night.

Smile

She didn't understand why that smile frightened her so much.

Even though she looked away, the clown's smile wouldn't leave her mind. To distract herself, she began to notice the other costumed figures. Mermaids, unicorns, brides... There were countless costumes, but none as striking as that one, with that smile.

It was Carnival, so she decided to enjoy herself. She sang, danced, jumped, drank, and laughed. Yet, in every carefree gesture, a part of her mind kept searching for the reason behind her discomfort.

Time passed, and the ghost of the clown haunting her mind began to fade. But before it disappeared completely, she caught a glimpse of the bright red tip of his hair standing out in the crowd.

She started trembling as she remembered that smile, even though she couldn't recall why it had scared her so much. She knew she couldn't keep pretending to be as cheerful as before. More than that, she felt she couldn't live without going after that clown.

Roberto Brecht

Unable to understand her own behavior, she pushed through the crowd, chasing that red tip. She reached the clown and stopped. Summoning all the courage she had, she broke through the paralysis beginning to take over her body and turned the creature with the terrifying smile around.

The man who looked back at her seemed confused. It was the same clown as before, but now there was no monster—just another ordinary person enjoying Carnival.

Relief washed over her, and she laughed.

The man laughed with her.

That smile! Something was wrong. It wasn't the smile of a human. His smile wasn't real; it was something terrifying, something that shouldn't exist. His mouth was too cruel, with teeth too sharp. A mouth that, in some way, belonged to a predator, someone who would kill for the pleasure of killing.

The monster returned. And with it, all the others.

She wasn't at a street party; everyone around her had terrifying fangs that would bite, tear, and kill her.

Desperation took over, and she ran for her life, screaming wildly.

Meanwhile, the revelers laughed at the woman running and screaming, but no one laughed harder than the man in the clown costume who was selling candy.

Roberto Brecht

Touch

After many months, this was the first time he had touched her.

It had always been the same way. In the middle of the night, he would wake up and gently run his hand through her hair. She would keep her eyes closed, but both knew it was part of their game.

After a few seconds, his fingers would trail down her back until she shivered. That was the signal for him to move his hand over the rest of her body.

It was cold, but they slept naked. This had started when they decided to have a child. Even though they gave up after a few years of trying, they kept the habit of sleeping without clothes.

His hand on her body began to awaken a warmth inside her that she hadn't felt in a long time— a warmth that overcame the cold of the room.

She felt him lightly biting her neck as he pulled her body closer to his.

Then his hand moved lower. The shock of that touch was greater than she had expected. She began to tremble as she lost control of her breathing.

Shot of Chaos

She knew what would happen next, yet she still gasped when he entered her. She moaned loudly as she caught her breath, something she hadn't done since her youth.

There was no more gentleness. They threw themselves at each other, holding on tightly. Even with her eyes closed, she was fully awake.

She couldn't remember the last time she had felt so much pleasure, trembling uncontrollably. The grinding of her teeth was only drowned out by her moans.

His breathing grew heavier. She knew what it meant. She couldn't hold on much longer either. It was the most intense orgasm of her life.

After what felt like an eternity of seconds, she regained control of her breathing. She struggled to stop trembling as her husband's icy body held her close.

The warmth she had felt inside her began to be replaced by a new coldness as reason returned. How could she be with her husband if he had passed away?

The icy arm that had held her let go. But that only sent a new chill through her body.

She took a deep breath and opened her eyes.

Seeing no one in the room was her breaking point.

Roberto Brecht

She wanted him back. And she cried at the thought of not being able to bear the loneliness anymore.

She didn't know yet, but loneliness no longer existed for her, now that a new life was growing inside her womb.

Love in the Time of the Plague

And it was in the time of the plague that love flourished.

Renato and Claudia were in the first months of a whirlwind romance when it arrived. Their desire grew, photos were exchanged until they started to look more and more alike. They had no choice but to talk and get to know each other. Love flourished.

Thiago and Mariana were siblings. They had spent 17 years nurturing a mutual hatred when it arrived. That day, Mariana cried. Thiago hugged her. Love flourished.

Valdemir and Luciana had been married for 15 years and were just two strangers when it arrived. With it came the first word in days. The first laugh. Together, they reminisced about the past, the joys and sorrows. Love flourished.

Pedro was disillusioned when it arrived. He downloaded a dating app and found Gustavo. Their eyes sparkled during the long conversations they had throughout the night. Love flourished.

Roberto Brecht

Joana was sure she would never forgive her father when it arrived. She still held a grudge when she heard his first dry cough. Concern arose. The grudge disappeared, care began, and the long-awaited apologies finally came. Love flourished.

Davi had never had anyone; he had lived on the streets for many years when it arrived. It was on a cold night that he met Fátima, a social worker who listened to him, fed him, and provided a dignified place for him to spend the next few months. Love flourished.

Luiz had been working as a doctor for many years when it arrived. He was tired but knew this would be his last mission before his long-awaited retirement. After another exhausting 14-hour shift, he gathered what little strength he had left for his last patient.

Immobilized, with little of her lung functioning, Sandra's tears flowed silently. Both knew nothing could be done to save her. With nothing to ease her pain, Luiz could only offer his compassion.

He looked into her eyes and froze. It took only a few seconds for an instant connection to form, and they recognized each other as equals, fighting with all their might for life.

As Luiz's tears began to fall, Sandra's tears stopped flowing.

Love flourished.

Change

Every change is hard, especially when you don't want to change anything.

She couldn't stop thinking about that as she felt the car sway at high speed. She had always loved traveling, but this was a journey she didn't want to take.

With her head down, she thought about what she was leaving behind. All she wanted was to continue with her life, or at least stay in the house she had lived in for so many years.

She felt like things had happened too fast. She hadn't even been able to prepare. She knew something would change, but by the time she realized it, she was already in the car, leaving behind everything she knew.

She looked out the window and was surprised. She thought it would be raining on such a sad day, but the setting sun turned the sky red. It was beautiful, but all she could associate that color with was blood.

For a few minutes, she had forgotten about her husband, who was still driving. She still didn't have the courage to talk to him. She was angry because he hadn't given her a choice. He had just packed their things, put her in the car, and now they were driving at 120 km/h in the opposite direction of what they had called home for years.

She returned to her thoughts. At the first opportunity, when the car stopped, she would get out and run back to her house. She laughed at the thought. It was impossible, and they both knew it.

The laughter faded, and sadness took its place. Even though she tried to hold back, she felt she couldn't control it anymore, and the first tear was about to fall.

Even without the courage to speak, she wanted her husband to notice what he had done. He would see her tears and know it was a mistake to change everything like this.

But before her own tears could fall, she noticed that, aside from his exhaustion, silent tears were streaming down her husband's face.

It was at that moment that she realized he had also left behind his home, his friends, his life.

They weren't prepared for the war, nor for the explosion, and certainly not for the life she was now forced to live without her legs.

That's why he had decided to run away. He would be considered a coward. But everything he did was for her.

Her tears finally fell.

Shot of Chaos

She took her husband's hand and felt that she hadn't abandoned anything. On the contrary, she had never been closer to home.

Roberto Brecht

Darkness

Since I was a child, I was never afraid of the dark, but of what it brought with it.

I don't remember the first time I heard them. Since then, they never left. They were voices, thousands of voices that surrounded me every time the lights went out. They came closer and closer until I could feel their breath, their smell, their touch. The noise became deafening, and at that point, no matter how much I tried to stay in control, I would panic until someone came with a light.

At first, my family and friends even joked by turning off the lights, but my desperation, and the marks they left, were real. Real enough for the jokes to stop in the first few years.

Time passed, and I learned to adapt. My phone was never out of battery. I always had candles and lighters at home in case the power went out. I even carried a flashlight in my bag at all times. Being in the dark was not an option in my life.

As an adult, I was convinced to seek help.

The scientist said it was all in my mind, but that didn't explain the scratches that appeared out of nowhere on my skin. The theologian only blamed me and made me pray, which was completely ineffective.

Either way, over time, I prepared so well that darkness no longer existed for me. I was never in places without light, and I didn't go anywhere with even the slightest possibility of darkness.

But these adaptations made them bolder. One day at dusk, I heard a voice in the distance. Even though it was unintelligible, I recognized pure hatred.

The first of many voices that grew closer each day. A candle at night was no longer enough to keep them away as before. Going out at night was no longer an option.

I became increasingly reclusive, a person surrounded daily by light. So much light that people began to suspect that what they called trauma was actually madness.

It only took one of those countless lights to go out, or a dark closet to open, for me to feel the hatred coming in waves and the voices, now screams, to begin. It was terrifying. I screamed back and protected myself with another layer of light.

They were waiting. When the first light went out, they would come for me with everything they had.

Even in extreme brightness, I could feel them now. Beneath all the layers of reality, I heard their voices in the background. I felt their hunger, but they still couldn't get closer.

Roberto Brecht

What I never imagined was that the same light that saved me for years would be my ruin. At least that's what the diagnosis said. Years of light only brought blindness that would grow worse day by day.

And now, for the first time in my life, it's me who waits. Desperate and resigned. With the darkness coming not from the outside in, but from the inside out, as the lights grow dimmer and the voices grow louder.

Vaccine

Despite the death of her son, she still didn't believe in vaccines.

She grew up in the city but had always been passionate about nature and the wisdom it offered. That's why she spent her entire life distrusting everything humanity produced. She was enlightened. Her connection to the universe was so strong that she could see what others couldn't and know what they didn't.

She wasn't foolish enough to believe in conspiracy theories, except when it came to the obvious schemes of big corporations that created diseases only to profit from their treatments. That's why she refused to put anything in her body that only served to make companies richer and would slowly kill her.

That's why, when her baby was born, she was adamant about refusing to vaccinate him.

The love she felt for her little one was so great that she was sure it, along with the teas she prepared, would be enough to cure him of the illness that had worsened since his birth.

Roberto Brecht

The day of his death was a shock to her life. She realized something was wrong. There was no lack of love or care, yet something hadn't been enough. So why would the universe take him from her?

Several days of grief passed until she realized that he had simply become one with the universe and that he would always be with her, helping her in her fight.

With that, her faith in nature was reinforced, as was her certainty that Western medicine was a fraud that needed to be eradicated.

She had an obligation to the truth, and she spread it to everyone through signs, posters, protests, and posts. She spoke with such certainty and love that she managed to open many people's eyes.

Her fight for the truth became a reference. Not even the high mortality rate among the children of those enlightened by her words could weaken her struggle. What was once dismissed by the medical community became a concern when children stopped being vaccinated on a large scale.

After years, she succeeded. Nature was valued again, and the medical fraud was exposed. Meanwhile, despite the pains of yellow fever, the enlightened woman smiled, knowing she would soon reunite with the universe and the son she had loved so much.

Secrecy

No one knew if it was hackers or the government itself, but what is known is that every conversation ever held online was leaked onto the internet.

All you needed was a name. With that, you could find every text, audio, and photo ever sent by anyone. Everything was recorded, and now, available for anyone to see. Impossible to delete or edit.

The shock society felt that day could be seen in the silence that swept through both the real and virtual worlds in the first few hours. Overnight, secrecy ceased to exist, and no one knew how to deal with it. Except for Jaime.

Jaime had never had anything to hide. From an early age, he knew how to handle his problems without ever seeking help. He was self-sufficient. That's why, when the news spread across the world, he was the only one who could lay his head on the pillow without the weight that crushed everyone else.

When he woke up, he turned on the TV, but there was nothing on. He went out for coffee, but nothing was open. Buses no longer ran; only hurried cars were on the streets.

Roberto Brecht

He decided to stay on his balcony, watching the street. People walked by with boxes in their hands, having been fired, heads hanging low. Couples screamed at each other. Children were kicked out of their homes. Fights and arguments broke out every minute. Secrets no longer existed, and with them, peace was gone.

Over the following days, the state of chaos persisted. Sins were exposed. Everyone was judged and condemned. The exception, once again, was Jaime, who had never left a trace.

A few months later, the internet was banned; it was too dangerous. It was the end of the digital world.

However, the minor offenses and confessions were not erased. Everyone was marked with a symbol of shame. Everyone except Jaime. Now seen as a saint in this new world that had reverted to the past century.

Over the years, everyone became so preoccupied with their own exposure that they stopped remembering the sins of others. And so they continued, guilty of crimes no one cared about anymore, simply accepting Jaime as someone to follow.

And Jaime, who had always hidden his secrets, reigned supreme. Never worrying about his own sins, which were too real to ever be written in the digital world.

Talisman

He was fascinated by his own future, and that was his biggest mistake.

He had always been obsessed with planning. He had ambitious goals, but not knowing if he would achieve them was frustrating.

Since then, he began to seek, in every possible way, to discover what would happen to him. Tarot, cowrie shells, crystal balls. But he knew the future they predicted wasn't real.

In parallel, he continued pursuing his ambitions. He achieved almost everything he set his mind to, yet he wasn't satisfied. He would go far, but not knowing how far was unbearable.

His search for the future continued as he advanced through the present. Achieving and growing.

Despite his search, it was on an ordinary day that he found the talisman that would change his future. He was walking down the street when his heart skipped a beat. He stopped and placed his hand on his chest, but what he felt was different from anything he had ever experienced in his life.

Roberto Brecht

Something was calling him. He began to sweat coldly as he walked in search of something he didn't know. He couldn't remember where he had been, only the sensation that led him to the abandoned house and the decrepit room where the talisman lay.

Touching the object made the sensation disappear. He had found it.

He took a deep breath, and the knowledge that the future he had sought for years was now in his hands took hold of his mind.

All he had to do was open the talisman. With the calm of a surgeon, he opened the object and looked inside.

His focused gaze turned into a smile. Then a laugh of happiness. There he was! Inside the talisman! He was old, but he was also where he had always wanted to be. He had all the success he had pursued for years. He would make it! He finally knew it! All his fears and uncertainties of the past years had been completely in vain!

He was still laughing when he looked at the talisman again. Without understanding what was happening, the truth began to take over his mind, and, trembling, he dropped the talisman, which shattered on the floor.

He abandoned the house and ran aimlessly, unable to stop thinking about the new image the talisman had shown him—a future where, knowing he could achieve everything, he achieved nothing but misery and loneliness.

Roberto Brecht

BDSM

Despite the pain he would feel, he knew this would be the best night of his life.

It had already been arranged. She would arrive at his house, and everything would be ready for the night they had both been waiting for.

Handcuffs, whips, ropes—they had tried it all. Each new experience was a new sensation, better than the last. The greater the pain, the greater the pleasure and happiness that lasted for days.

Unfortunately, with time, routine returned, and with it, unhappiness.

The only thing that kept him going was the thought that they would meet again and that happiness would once again be present in his life.

As he prepared everything, he remembered the past few months. How things had evolved. It started with something light, and before they knew it, they were doing things they had never imagined. Interestingly, the respect between them only grew, and their relationship was stronger than ever.

And today, they would finally reach the limit. They had talked a lot about it. It was as if the past few months had been just preparation for this night.

Shot of Chaos

He lost his breath when she arrived. She was stunning. Powerful. He was sure she could do whatever she wanted with him. She took his hand and led him to the bedroom.

When the first pain came, he knew the night he had longed for had begun. With a loving coldness, she tortured him.

He felt his face burn. The blindfold prevented him from knowing where the next pain would come from. Yet, the smile never left his face.

The moment he had been waiting for was near. He felt her hands on his neck. She squeezed as he thought his happiness couldn't be greater.

In a few seconds, it would all be over. That entire journey through pain would turn into a happiness he had never felt before.

She continued to squeeze his neck. His breath began to fade. It wouldn't be long now.

Just as he was about to pass out, she let go. Gasping, he looked into her eyes and felt that the love between them was at its peak.

It was time for what he had been waiting for. Finally, he spoke:

"Will you marry me?"

The sparkle in her eyes said it all. It was a yes!

And from that day on, happiness never left them again.

Roberto Brecht

Loneliness

The diagnosis came just a few days before the quarantine. Schizophrenia intensified by stress. It's funny to think that until recently, I saw the hallucinations as something natural, but after being convinced to seek an explanation, I began to fear that an episode could happen at any moment.

Few people knew about my condition; there was no reason for alarm. Small things happened, but generally nothing that made me worry. That's why, when the quarantine became a reality, I imagined it would be an important period to clear my head and relax.

Unfortunately, I couldn't have been more wrong.

The first day began with buying the essentials for a long period without contact with the outside world. My savings were enough, and despite the suspension of my work contract, I knew that once the pandemic normalized, my job would be secure. I spent the day organizing everything I needed for a month of comfort and self-discovery. I was tired when I went to bed, but the satisfaction was complete.

I woke up feeling like I was on vacation. After lying in bed for a while, I checked my social media. I didn't understand the concern of some friends. I wasn't ignoring the situation of vulnerable people—many didn't have savings and needed all the help they could get—but that wasn't the case for the friends who shared their worries about the virus and the quarantine.

I knew I wouldn't relax if I stayed connected. I put my phone aside and picked up one of the many books I had been putting off reading for years. After a few minutes, I realized I hadn't made it past the first paragraph.

I shouldn't have read what my friends posted. Their negativity affected me, as did thinking about the people who had no choice but to expose themselves to the virus. I had done my part; the food I donated would be enough to feed a few families. Besides, what else could I do?

I needed to stop thinking about it. Having a guilty conscience wasn't part of my ideal isolation. I tried to read again, and to my surprise, this time the reading flowed.

I woke up the next day and didn't check social media. It wasn't that I didn't care about my friends, but I believed isolation would be beneficial. It was a good day. I was so motivated that, without realizing it, the ingredients I had set aside in the sink turned into the cake I had been planning to make for months. I watched the movies on my list and started a new series without worrying about the number of episodes.

Another day passed, and then another. More movies, more books, more recipes, more series. Slowly, I realized that the more I had, the less I felt.

I woke up, and the will to get out of bed took a while to come. After some time listening to the sound of birds, I decided it was time to find out what was happening outside my home.

The first deaths were being reported. When the quarantine began, we knew it was only a matter of time before deaths started, but the hope that the distance from the epicenter of the disease and the tropical climate would make our country's reality different still lingered.

There was no point in dwelling on it. The virus would run its course, and all I could do was continue isolating myself. To distract myself, I did some exercises. Despite the limited space, moving my body brought an energy I hadn't felt in days. The sensation of water running down my body made me forget everything as I showered and reflected on the deaths. It took me a few minutes to realize the shower was off.

I had turned on the shower and felt the warmth of the water on my body. I had no doubt about that. I turned the shower on again and continued my bath. Only when I was drying off did I remember the diagnosis. Schizophrenia intensified by stress.

Shot of Chaos

That didn't make sense. There was no reason for stress. Even with the pandemic, I was at home in considerable comfort. I convinced myself that I had just been confused and soon forgot about it.

Another day. Another movie. A boring series. Food that lost its flavor. The exercise didn't lift my spirits. The book was illegible. It would have been a completely forgettable day, except for the scare I got.

It was late at night when, just as I was about to fall asleep, I heard a loud thud from outside. I jumped up and, after a few paralyzed seconds, ran to the window. A bird was dead outside. It had hit the window with such force that the glass was cracked. I thought about opening the window and picking up the bird, but what would I do with a dead bird inside the house?

Once again, I felt powerless. I left the bird where it was and decided I wouldn't worry about it that day. I didn't need another problem.

When I woke up the next day, I had forgotten about the bird. I only remembered it in the middle of the afternoon when I opened the window to get some sun. It was the second scare the bird gave me—first with the thud, now with the complete lack of any trace of its existence. Even the window was fixed.

Before I could worry, I realized it had all been a dream. Realizing that made me laugh for the first time in days. I needed to have more fun.

Roberto Brecht

Boredom grew with each passing day. That's why I spent a few hours every day looking at the empty streets. I stuck my face out the window and felt the wind and the sun. How I had missed that! I also watched the street; very few people were out. If it weren't for the countless delivery drivers on bikes and motorcycles, I would have thought a genocide had happened.

Watching them made me miss eating something I hadn't made myself. I needed a moment of happiness, even if fleeting. Despite the promise I had made to avoid contact with the outside world, I decided to make an exception and order a dessert or something close to what I would eat if I could go out.

I opened a delivery app and chose my favorite pie. I was happy to find it because I had heard that the restaurant that made it would close during the pandemic. A few minutes later, the doorbell rang. As requested, I waited for the delivery driver to go down the stairs and leave the building before opening the door.

My surprise was immense when I faced the empty hallway. No neighbor could have taken the pie in that short time. Surely, the delivery driver had taken the pie for himself and assumed I would blame the neighbors. I opened the app and decided to complain to the restaurant, but no matter how much I searched, I couldn't find it anymore.

Schizophrenia intensified by stress. Those words echoed in my mind as I focused all my energy on rationally explaining what had happened. It took me a while to believe it was just a big coincidence and that the restaurant had deleted its account on the app between the time I placed the order and the driver's theft of the pie.

The following hours were agonizing. Without the pie and with nothing to lift my spirits, I slowly realized that isolation wasn't doing me any good. For the second time during the entire quarantine, I turned on the TV for news, and what I saw terrified me. The deaths, which had been close to zero before, were now in the hundreds. The virus was spreading across the country, and the government seemed unable to agree on how to handle the situation.

Hundreds dead, thousands infected. How was this possible? It had only been a few days since the first deaths. I thought it would be different here, but if the virus had grown so much in recent days, what would the next days be like? How were my friends? How was everyone?

I opened social media, and the situation was even more desperate. My friends were fine, but their acquaintances were starting to get infected. It was as if the virus was getting closer every day.

I needed air. I opened the window, and what I saw scared me more than the news. People were on the streets. People were on the streets! Not as many as before the pandemic, but far more than in the early days when I only saw delivery drivers. The urge to yell at them arose, but I managed to control myself in time. I couldn't lose control.

I closed the window and lay down. Hours passed as thousands of thoughts danced through my mind. It was the first of many sleepless nights.

The singing of the birds made me realize it was dawn, and even a sleepless night didn't help me resolve the dilemma between staying in my bubble or seeking information. Isolation seemed both terrifying and tempting at the same time. Since I couldn't reach a solution, I deleted social media from my phone. That at least would keep me from giving in to temptation.

The mere idea of watching something was inconceivable, as was trying to read or cook. All I wanted was to lie down, sleep, and wake up at the end of this crisis. I needed to do something before the despair became uncontrollable. The only thing I managed to do was cry, which helped me relieve some of the tension I was feeling.

I no longer looked out the window. The thought of seeing people on the streets while the virus was loose filled me with anguish. Over time, day and night blurred together. I spent hours and hours awake, knowing I needed to sleep but unable to.

I woke up to someone calling me. I pressed my face into the pillow and tried to block out the sounds. Schizophrenia intensified by stress.

Shot of Chaos

I was definitely stressed; there was no denying that. I knew that if I waited long enough, the hallucination would go away, and I could convince myself, once again, that it had never existed.

The voice kept calling me. Insistently. Knocks on the door.

It wasn't going away. Waiting wouldn't help. I had to do something.

I got up and went to the door. I knew what would happen. I would open the door, and there would be nothing on the other side. That would drive me even crazier, but when I faced the truth, the sound would stop.

I put the key in the lock when I heard the voice on the other side of the door.

"Neighbor, you don't need to open the door! I just wanted to know if you're okay. I haven't heard anything from your apartment in a few days, and I got worried."

"Don't worry, I'm fine! I've been reading these past few days and ended up quieter than usual," I replied, trying to keep my voice normal.

"I'm so sorry! I didn't mean to bother you, but in these pandemic times, we have to look out for each other. I'll let you get back to your reading. If you need anything, just let me know! I live in apartment 43!"

I listened to his footsteps down the hallway as I sat on the floor with my back against the door. I took a deep breath as a strange sensation took over my body.

After so long without contact with another human, I finally felt something close to motivation. That night, I could taste my food again and relax with a movie. It seemed like the first step on a journey back to normalcy.

The next day went like the first few days. I woke up late and lingered in bed while checking my social media. I had a vague memory of thinking about deleting them, but the memory came and went just as quickly. Looking at my friends' photos made me miss them. Tonight, I would call one of them and make plans. In the meantime, I kept scrolling through photos of beaches and parties I had missed.

I couldn't remember the last time I had been so excited. I sang and danced in the shower while imagining the trip I had planned for the end of the year. It would be 20 days of parties and fun, far from the stress of work and city life.

I got out of the shower and got dressed, but something didn't feel right. I knew I was on leave, but I couldn't remember exactly why. I thought about going out for a drink, but the feeling that something was wrong wouldn't leave me. I shouldn't leave the house. I laughed at the thought that it might be a premonition.

Shot of Chaos

I was still laughing when I heard my best friend's voice. I froze. He had probably heard me singing in the shower. He would probably laugh about it for years. Either way, I followed his voice and found him sitting on the living room couch.

As always, the conversation was great. He told me about his promotion at work and his new girlfriend. I was happy for him because I had been rooting for both things to happen in his life for a long time.

But when it was my turn, I didn't know what to say. It was as if nothing new was happening in my life. As if I were stuck in time while everyone else's lives moved forward.

After a lot of talking, we decided to watch an old movie, like we had done many times when we were teenagers. Without realizing it, I fell asleep and woke up with a start.

What was happening? For a minute, I didn't recognize my own home. It was as if I were lying in some unfamiliar place. Slowly, things began to make more sense, until I finally realized I was alone in my room, lying in my bed.

I looked at my phone and remembered it wasn't a good idea. Knowing about the pandemic wouldn't make me feel better. I left it on the bed and got up. I needed a shower.

Roberto Brecht

Hours passed as I killed time with activities I could no longer stand. With a lot of willpower, I managed to read. It was the first book I had read during the entire pandemic, so I felt proud when I closed the last page. A small victory after many days. So many days. I started to wonder how many days.

There was no way to know how much time had passed, not without reconnecting with the outside world. Despite my fear, I took my phone out of my pocket and automatically opened the browser.

Thousands. We were at thousands of deaths. I don't remember if I even saw the date, and if I did, it didn't matter anymore. There were thousands of deaths in my country and millions infected worldwide. Millions infected.

I needed to stop reading those news stories. My breathing faltered as I heard the diagnosis echoing in my mind again. Schizophrenia intensified by stress. It had been years since I had seen anything unusual, but the stress the news caused me was so profound that I was afraid I might start hallucinating again, and worse, that isolation would prevent me from realizing a hallucination had happened.

Without thinking, I threw the phone against the wall with force and heard it shatter. I laughed at the thought that my neighbor would hear the noise and no longer think I had died. That laugh turned into a full-blown fit of laughter. I couldn't control myself; my stomach hurt, and I thought I would fall to the floor from laughing so hard. With tears in my eyes, I got up and, still laughing, went to the kitchen.

Cooking always made me feel better. During the process, I only thought about the ingredients, flavors, smells, and seasonings. I came up with a recipe in my head and was willing to try something new. I started gathering the ingredients when I noticed how little food I had in my kitchen. I had made a large enough purchase to feed myself for a long time.

I even considered that the food might have been stolen, but that couldn't have happened since I had been home the whole time. At the same time, I was sure I hadn't eaten that much during the quarantine.

Either way, I was determined to create this dish. I ended up focusing on its preparation, and the mystery of the missing food faded from my mind as the meal came together. The evening was pleasant. I drank a glass of wine and ate well. The flavor was back.

As I lay down, I began to reflect on the singing of the birds, which, like the virus, had grown exponentially over the past few days. Before the pandemic, I had never noticed that sound, but now, it seemed never to go away. I fell asleep realizing that I was becoming more and more like a bird trapped in a cage.

Roberto Brecht

I woke up feeling motivated. The flavor from the previous day was still lingering in my life. I went to the window and opened it for the first time in a long while. The cold wind hit my face as I took in the smells the night had brought. It was the most pleasant sensation I had felt since the beginning of the quarantine.

A smile began to form as I finally looked down. People. So many people. I didn't know what to make of it; I just felt the strange sensation that took over my stomach. The cold that touched my face seemed to seep inside my body as I slowly stepped away from the window.

Gradually, the cold I felt began to turn into heat. I couldn't let this happen. Maybe I was wrong. The pandemic could have ended, and I was the only one who didn't know! It was a remote possibility, but a possibility nonetheless. I clung to it tightly as I searched for my phone on the bed.

The news was terrifying. Deaths continued to rise exponentially, but worse than that was the government's neglect, which had clearly given up fighting the virus and now accepted deaths as something inevitable. In the name of the economy, the government was pushing people to risk their lives, as if it were possible to return to normal.

I began to tremble with anger. They were supposed to protect us; that's what they were there for! Now they were going the opposite way to "save the country's economy"?

The rage consumed me. I wanted to scream. I wanted to fight. I couldn't let them do this! We couldn't let them!

Thinking about "us" made me remember my friends, and fear took the place of anger. I realized that since the quarantine began, I hadn't spoken to any of them. Without thinking about whether it would be good or bad for me, I opened social media. I needed to know how they were. I needed to make sure they were okay.

Time stopped as I stared at my phone screen.

Mourning. What do you mean, mourning? It couldn't be real.

My oldest friend was gone. Another victim of the virus. Another "inevitable" death to ensure the well-being of the country's economy.

He was young! He was young! How could he have died? I couldn't accept it! He died, and I didn't save him! I could have convinced him to stay home; I could have invited him to spend the days here. I could have, but I did nothing. I just isolated myself and didn't help anyone.

I needed to get out of that house. I needed someone. I needed a hug. I couldn't bear that pain alone.

Roberto Brecht

Without thinking about what to do or say, I left my apartment for the first time and walked down the empty hallway to apartment 43. My neighbor didn't need to open the door; I just needed him to talk to me. That was all I needed—the slightest human contact.

I knocked on the door when I realized I didn't know the neighbor's name. That didn't matter now; I needed someone, and he was the only one who had shown even the slightest concern for me during all this time. I knocked again.

Silence.

This time, I was the one who got worried. Was he another victim of the virus? I wasn't going to lose anyone else, not even a neighbor whose name I didn't know. I seemed like a madman, but I kept knocking on the door and shouting. I tried to turn the doorknob and, to my surprise, the door was unlocked.

I opened the door a few inches while calling out for the neighbor. A strange smell emerged. I didn't want to invade his space, just as the fear of catching the virus stopped me from taking another step. I called out again. No response. What if he was unconscious, or worse, dead? I needed to find out.

In one motion, I opened the rest of the door and found myself facing an empty apartment. I tried to focus on breathing, but it was getting harder and harder. There was no sign of furniture or that anyone had lived in that apartment for some time.

Shot of Chaos

There was an explanation: he had probably moved during the quarantine. That explained his absence, but not the dust that seemed to have accumulated for at least six months.

I didn't want to stay in that place any longer. Confused, I returned to my apartment while trying to understand what was happening.

Once again, that voice reminded me of the diagnosis that explained everything. Schizophrenia intensified by stress.

That's not it. I know I can have hallucinations, but I know myself. I know what's real and what's not. I'm not crazy. I just need to rest, and tomorrow everything will make sense.

But no matter how hard I tried, I couldn't rest. Now, the sound of the birds was becoming deafening, but I didn't care anymore. I lay there, apathetic, for longer than I could quantify. The death of my friend or the imminence of my madness seemed insignificant. I just waited, as if time and the future would bring something new.

I no longer had hope. I didn't think. I didn't cry. I just let time pass.

I had my eyes closed when I felt a gentle hand on my hair. The birds fell silent for the first time in days.

Roberto Brecht

For a second, I thought my friend's spirit had returned to blame me for his death, but not even that thought made me react.

Deep down, I knew it wasn't him. I knew that hand, that touch, those movements. I had felt them since the day I was born.

I opened my eyes and saw my mother smiling beside me.

I hugged her, and all the pain and anguish I had accumulated exploded. Desperate tears streamed down uncontrollably as I sobbed in her lap.

She continued to stroke my hair while softly saying my name. I felt her affection as something almost tangible. The sadness faded, and in its place remained love.

I lifted my face and looked at her. Despite the tears still falling, I was now smiling.

Almost embarrassed, she began apologizing for not being able to keep her promise to stay at home. Little did she know that it was her breaking that promise that saved me.

Even with all the gratitude I felt for her being with me, I couldn't accept that she had risked herself just to see me. I thought about scolding her, but I still didn't have the strength for that. Instead, I quietly told her she didn't need to have come.

She laughed in her carefree way, as she often did when I showed concern. She knew how to calm me down. It was as if she had a sixth sense that told her when I needed help, and she always appeared in my worst moments.

As if in slow motion, she stood up and pulled me with her. I felt like a child again as she led me to the living room. We sat side by side, and she began telling me about her recent days. She said she and my father were doing well and hadn't left the house once. She had made progress on her recipe book and finally fixed the roof problem that had been postponed for so many years.

Before I knew it, we were engaged in a lively conversation about the past, reminiscing for the thousandth time the same old stories. And, as always, it was a pleasure to talk about them.

How I loved that woman. Her eyes sparkled as we relived our past. She made me forget the pain, the death, the madness, and the virus plaguing the world.

After hours and hours of conversation, she finally stood up. It was time to go. I couldn't hold back the tears, but I promised I would be strong.

As suddenly as she had arrived, she was gone, and I found myself alone again. Leaving me only with the memory of her presence and a longing that tightened my chest. It wasn't the best feeling, but it was better than the apathy that had weighed on me until then.

Roberto Brecht

I wouldn't break the promise. I got out of bed and went to take a shower. It was comforting to stand under the water, letting my tears mix with the falling stream. I had decided to be strong.

It was dawn when I got out of the shower. My stomach growled as if I were starving. Looking closely, I thought I had lost weight, even though I cooked every day.

I opened the cupboard and found more food than I remembered from the last time. The fridge was also full, and despite the faint smell of spoiled food, everything seemed to be in order. I searched for the source of the smell, but it seemed to be spread throughout the house.

In the sink was a half-empty glass of milk. I didn't remember when I had poured it—probably before the shower. I looked at it carefully, but nothing seemed off. I turned the glass and, despite the slightly sour taste, drank it all at once, as if I hadn't had anything to drink in days.

I sat in the living room while reflecting on the past few days. I remembered my mother, feeling sad, an empty house, my broken phone on the floor... but everything was so confusing, just fragments that didn't fit together. The only things clear in my mind were the virus and the diagnosis. Schizophrenia intensified by stress.

There was no more to think about the virus. It would be the end of everything I knew, and whether or not I was crazy wouldn't change that. There was no more hope. Acceptance was necessary.

I tried to get up from the couch, but dizziness hit me, and I ended up falling to the floor. My stomach hurt, and I felt extremely weak. No matter how hard I tried, I couldn't get up. It was as if gravity had grown stronger and was pushing me down. My face was pressed against the floor, and I felt like my skull would crack if this continued.

I was paralyzed. Just as my mother hadn't kept her promise to stay at home, I wouldn't keep my promise to be strong. There was no more energy in my body, no more pain. Nothing existed except acceptance.

A knock at the door.

I couldn't move. I just lay there, my face turned toward the door. I could clearly see the doorknob turning as I watched it shake with increasingly forceful knocks. Beyond the sound of the pounding, there was another indecipherable noise, like thousands of voices screaming at once.

Unable to close my eyes, I watched the shadow that crept inch by inch under the door, slowly moving toward me. It was the virus. It would enter through my nose and be the end of everything.

Knowing the virus would kill me made acceptance fade away, while despair took over my being. I didn't want to die. Yet, that wasn't enough to make me move when the door violently swung open.

Roberto Brecht

I still hoped my mother would appear and save me again, but that's not what happened. Instead of my beloved mother, thousands of birds burst into my house at once, with a sound so loud I couldn't hear my own screams.

They pecked and scratched me as the virus took over my body, squeezing me, strangling me, and entering inside me.

I couldn't breathe, I couldn't scream anymore. The pain I hadn't felt in days returned all at once, and darkness slowly took over.

It took me some time to orient myself when I finally opened my eyes. I wasn't in my room. The open window made the curtain sway gently as the sunlight hit my face directly. Almost inaudibly, I could hear the distant sound of birds.

- Finally, you're awake! – said a familiar voice. – I thought you were dead when I found you. We tried calling you countless times, but we only discovered your phone was broken when I found you.

I was still staring in shock at the man speaking from the doorway when he continued.

- Sorry, I guess you don't remember me. My name is Ricardo, the neighbor who knocked on your door a few months ago. We thought you had moved away! No one in our building knew anything about you. You can't imagine the surprise of finding you in that state!

I tried to speak, but it was impossible. My throat hurt as if I hadn't used it in months. At that moment, a man in white appeared, spoke quickly with Ricardo, and hurried away. Ricardo continued.

- Don't worry, I'm doing my residency at this hospital, and I've already taken care of the paperwork. We'll take care of you here until you're better. I also took the liberty of calling your mother and letting her know you're with us. She should be catching a flight in the next few days and will stay with you during your recovery.

I believe my worried look was enough for him to understand and respond.

- It's true, maybe you don't know this, but we've finally found a vaccine for the virus! In fact, the quarantine is being relaxed as we immunize the population. So, don't worry, your mother won't be at risk when she meets you.

I took a deep breath as relief washed over me. The confusion in my mind began to dissolve as hope returned.

- I see this news has cured you more than the medicine we gave you. – said Ricardo with a smile – Now rest. I'll come back to see you tomorrow.

Ricardo left and I was alone in the room. I didn't have the physical or mental strength to understand what had happened. I only knew I wouldn't need to worry anymore, after all, the greatest stress of my life was over.

Outside my mind, the battle continued.

With fewer and fewer people respecting the quarantine, the virus was spreading rapidly. The government still didn't know how to control the situation, and deaths were multiplying. Social chaos was approaching.

Meanwhile, I remained alone. Unconsciously knowing that my broken mind was the same one that saved me, by giving me something no one else had at that moment.

Hope.

Father and Daughter

"You need to let me go."

Hearing those words hurt, especially because he knew they were true.

He had always been a protective father, but in recent years, his relationship with his daughter had changed completely.

One day, he asked her to stay home more. Then he asked her to come back early. Before they knew it, she no longer left the house and stopped seeing everyone except him.

Yet, there were no demands. He didn't force her to stay. He'd simply look at her, and she knew he wanted her close.

At first, she didn't mind. Her father was the great love of her life, and she wouldn't abandon him in his fragile state.

Years passed, and their love remained as strong as ever. Still, he sensed something was wrong.

Roberto Brecht

He slowly realized the bond between them wasn't enough for her. But nothing prepared him for the day she spoke those painful words.

That day, she stared out the window for hours, as she'd done for months. But for the first time, he saw a tear roll down her cheek.

He hadn't seen her cry since the accident—not since it took her life and left him paraplegic.

Then she said he needed to let her go.

He froze, turned his wheelchair, and retreated to his room, weeping. He knew this day would come, but he didn't know how to live without her.

He was old, weak, and broken. Worse, without her, he'd lose the last source of love in his life.

Minutes later, his daughter entered the room and hugged him.

Feeling her embrace, he sobbed uncontrollably.

He couldn't understand how this was possible. Since the accident that killed her and paralyzed him, they'd never touched. Yet here she was.

He looked at her one last time before she slowly faded away.

But instead of emptiness, he felt something new.

Then he understood how she'd hugged him.

Shot of Chaos

Her final act was leaving him all the love she had—
the last thread tying her to this world and the father
she loved so deeply.

Roberto Brecht

Quantum Coaching

It had been intense weeks, but now he was officially a Quantum Coach! It was time to use his knowledge to improve people's lives.

He knew the secret: he understood the law of attraction. The universe gives back what we ask of it. More than just a coach, he was an expert in quantum physics and biology. DNA was in his hands to reprogram it for those in need.

He saw people suffering from cancer, depression, and knew that if they were on the right frequency, all of it would disappear. Thankfully, he could help—with the right guidance, anyone could achieve physical, mental, spiritual, and financial health.

At one point, he considered getting a psychology degree. Now he saw that as a waste of time.

With this confidence, he began his practice. Bankrupt clients, sick clients. In just a few sessions, he could channel the energy needed for the coveted quantum leap. But this was a two-way street, and when results faltered, he blamed their lack of willpower.

Then, between appointments, he met Mariana. She was desperate. Her daughter needed help, and he was the perfect person for it. Promising quick improvement, he began the sessions.

Week after week, he tried, but the girl wouldn't "effort." She stayed quiet, apathetic. Strange. No matter what he did, she seemed immune to his vibrations. He tried to "change her frequency", pointing out what she needed to do, but each session left her more distant.

Mariana, however, believed every word. No psychologist was needed—he convinced her they'd soon "break through that shell" and realign what was out of order.

At the next session, Mariana walked into his office. As promised, the shell broke. Mariana discovered this when she found her daughter dead that morning.

The coach tried to blame the girl's weakness, but the news shattered his illusions.

No matter how hard he "manifested positivity," the universe didn't respond.

He needed help.

He needed a psychologist.

Roberto Brecht

Torture

It was the fifth straight day of being tortured without knowing why.

It all started on an ordinary day. He left home for work but never made it to the bus stop. A black van pulled up in front of him, and armed men forced him inside.

That's when his nightmare began. He thought it was a kidnapping and tried to negotiate, but the moment he opened his mouth, the first blow landed.

The taste of blood filled his mouth, and he thought he'd pass out. Little did he know that punch would be nothing compared to what awaited him in the coming days.

He was blindfolded but sensed the van stopping. He was shoved into what he assumed was a room and tied to a chair. His clothes were torn off, and aside from distant screams, he felt utterly alone.

He was terrified, tears streaming endlessly. He didn't know why he was there or who these people were.

After hours, the blindfold was removed, and he faced a blinding light. They began shouting at him:

Shot of Chaos

"Terrorist! Communist! Thug! Murderer!" He was part of a conspiracy he'd never heard of until now.

He tried to speak, but they didn't want answers. More blows. Everywhere. He blacked out.

He woke up screaming. Electric shocks surged through his body. He couldn't breathe. The pain was beyond words.

The accusations resumed. Every time he tried to speak, the torture restarted—more inventive, more brutal. He'd give them anything, but he had nothing.

Days blurred into cycles of pain and unconsciousness: punches, shocks, cuts, drownings, threats against his family.

He tried to hold onto hope, but it was impossible. He had no strength left to scream. No will to explain. The air grew heavier, the darkness thicker, death closer.

Then he noticed the screams that had haunted him since day one were gone. The pain vanished.

The next day, his photo spread nationwide, accompanied by news that the terrorist leader had killed himself before capture.

Roberto Brecht

Faith

Her faith was unshakable, and she made sure to show it.

But it wasn't always this way. For a long time, she believed quietly, like many others—privately, at home. She thought she didn't need the church, that her love for God was enough.

This lasted until her first invitation to a service. The moment she entered the church, she noticed the congregants' stares. Her clothes, her demeanor, her speech—everything was judged.

The experience was crushing, and she left worse than she arrived. That's when she vowed never to endure that again.

The following week, she returned to the same service. But now, the stares were different. Her hair was tied up, her clothes modest, her gestures restrained and subtle. No one would ever question her love for God again.

To ensure this, she distanced herself from "worldly" things. She wanted no temptations. Secular music was replaced with gospel; her old clothes discarded. Faith and God became her sole focus.

Shot of Chaos

The Bible, once merely important, became her only moral compass.

Soon, she became a beacon of "faith's power"—her church's pride, a model to emulate.

In the name of faith, she preached her discovered "truth." So, she turned her gaze outward. Sin ruled the world, and she couldn't ignore it.

Based on the Bible, she preached love. Based on the Bible, she preached hate. Her prejudices were all justified with handpicked verses.

She stopped being the judged and became the judge, dividing the world into "sinners deserving scorn" and "the chosen."

Day by day, she drew closer to her God, certain of His eternal love awaiting her.

What she didn't realize was that her true god watched intently, celebrating every act, patiently awaiting the day they'd meet—and she'd receive all the "love" of his eternal flames.

Roberto Brecht

Best Friend

Some friendships are so intense they become suffocating.

I've never been one to have many friends. Truthfully, I'd never had any. Something inside me kept me from opening up or trusting people. But with Paulo, it was friendship at first sight.

I was jogging in the park when I first saw him. He was jogging too. We exchanged a "good morning," and an hour later, we were laughing together on a park bench. How that greeting turned into hours of conversation, I'll never know. I just know it was mutual.

In the days that followed, we jogged together every morning. It was effortless to be around him. Soon, jogs turned into lunches, dinners, and increasingly frequent meetups. We were inseparable.

Before I knew it, there was nothing about my life Paulo didn't know. I trusted him completely and, for the first time, fully surrendered to a friendship.

I only felt whole when we were together. I loved hearing about his life—how his day went, who he talked to, who he went out with. But things began to shift.

Shot of Chaos

I remember waiting for him at the square where we'd met for nearly an hour. I called repeatedly but ended up jogging alone that day. When he finally answered, he claimed he was sick. I knew right then something was wrong.

The next day, he was "better," and we jogged together. But the way he avoided my eyes told me everything.

Over the weeks, he grew more distant. I insisted there was no need for lies—we were friends and could tell each other anything. But he kept denying it. Still, I couldn't ignore how little I mattered to him now.

One day, Paulo canceled lunch. Then he stopped answering my calls.

I tried everything to understand, but he ignored me more each day. Until I got one final text: "Stop contacting me."

According to Paulo, I was suffocating him.

What Paulo didn't know was that our friendship wasn't something I could let go. He meant too much to me.

That's why I went to his house. That's why I begged. That's why I screamed.

That's why I suffocated him.

Now I jog alone, grieving the truth: Paulo will never run with me again.

Roberto Brecht

Birthday

For the tenth time that day, Catharina feared no one would come to her birthday party.

A foolish fear. She had great friends and knew this would never happen to her. Still, she sped up the car to ensure no one arrived before she got home.

When she finally arrived, she relaxed. She hadn't needed to rush. Everything was just as she'd left it before work. At least she could rest until the guests arrived.

She lay on the couch but couldn't sleep. Restless, uneasy. She stood up, pacing the decorated room, glancing at the wall clock.

Minutes dragged like hours, but finally, it was 7 PM! Her friends would arrive any moment. She couldn't wait any longer. She paced back and forth, smiling at the thought of the night ahead.

By 7:45 PM, worry crept in, but she reminded herself people always run late.

At 8:15 PM, she grew nervous, forcing herself to believe such delays were normal.

By 9 PM, she was furious. No one had shown up! No calls! No one!?

Shot of Chaos

Wait—a car pulled up. She rushed to the window. It was her best friend! She waited, irritation fading into hope. She rehearsed what she'd say when he knocked. But he never got out… He drove away!

She couldn't believe it. He must've seen no one else and didn't want to be alone. She paced faster, angrier.

At 10:15 PM, the phone rang. She lunged for it, recognizing her friend's voice—sobbing on the other end. Probably an excuse. Catharina didn't care. She screamed, but her friend hung up after seconds.

No longer angry, Catharina collapsed to the floor, sobbing uncontrollably, unaware she hadn't tired despite hours of pacing.

Roberto Brecht

Revelation

For years, his heart hadn't raced like this—fast, pounding, alive. Yet his stomach was ice-cold and hollow. One moment he felt heat, the next chill, his body betraying him in conflicting waves.

Ten minutes left. He knew every dilemma of his life would flood his mind in these final moments. He'd expected it, but not this intensity.

He tried to think rationally. He could still back out. Explain things. But deep down, he wouldn't quit now—not after coming this far. Even if it meant hell.

Nothing about this was rational. Nine minutes left. How could he not think?

He studied the room: a generic hotel suite, except for the clock above the door. In 28 years, he'd never seen a hotel clock placed there. Coincidence? No. Coincidences didn't exist—only divine will. This was God's design: the clock, the room, his damnation in seven and a half minutes.

Twenty-eight years without faltering. Twenty-eight years resisting temptations he'd never imagined. Always steadfast, devoted. Why today? Why this?

He checked the clock again. Seven minutes. Unless she arrived early. His stomach froze. He'd never touched anyone—never kissed, never… that. Sacred thoughts dissolved. Sweat dripped down his face. He'd fail. He knew it.

Was this God's will? Maybe the call, the temptation—all a test.

Footsteps outside. Not hers, but his heart lurched. He trembled, numb. Tears streamed—not sweat, but rage. Rage at himself. He'd lose his congregation, his future wife, his children. He could lie, but that'd make the sin worse.

Two minutes. Heat replaced cold. He stood, pacing like a madman—a sinner, unworthy.

The doorknob turned.

The woman entered, read his panic, and wordlessly pushed him onto the bed. No words needed.

He closed his eyes. With every second, he felt God slipping away.

His pants slid off. Tears returned—shame this time.

Then her touch: warm, gentle. Good.

Gentleness turned urgent. His breath hitched. She straddled him, and his heart stopped. He was inside her.

In that moment, he knew he wouldn't go to hell. After all, he'd finally met his one true God.

Roberto Brecht

Howl

He was still young but had been on the streets long enough to forget he'd once had a family.

So long that he no longer noticed how degrading his life was. Wake, walk, eat whatever he found, walk more, feel hunger, sleep. Days blurred into sameness. No surprises.

People were cruel, so he trusted no one. He grew quieter, more withdrawn. His loneliness was so deep his own company sufficed.

Years of routine turned him into something to hide—less than alive, a shadow-thing undeserving of sharing space with those who belonged in the city.

That's why the man's call startled him: not just food, but rarer still—kindness. After so long, he couldn't refuse either.

He ate until he sickened. This pain was worse. Desperate, he staggered back to the only one who'd shown him care in years.

His hope was met with a snarl of hatred. How dare he beg for help?

Before he could react, the man raised a gleaming metal rod. He tried to flee—weak, slow.

Shot of Chaos

The first strike. Pain. Blood. He scrambled up, legs buckling. Broken.

Blow after blow. New agony layered over old. Eventually, he felt nothing—just the thud-thud of steel and the warm seep of blood. He stopped fighting. The man was right. He should have given up.

Time blurred. Alone again. Bleeding on pavement, ignored by passersby.

In his final seconds, his tail stopped twitching. As if to mark his farewell, he opened his mouth—for the first time in years—and released one last, mournful howl.

Roberto Brecht

Final Dose

I should have left with you.

Looking back, I don't know how we grew close—but now, I can't imagine life without you.

That's why your leaving shattered me. One day, we were laughing like we always did, and the next, you were gone.

You'd warned me this would happen. I can't blame you. Still, I wasn't ready.

Months of preparation, months of jokes. Now, alone, I regret not cherishing our time.

I promised I wouldn't mourn your leaving, but I miss you. So much that I want to abandon everything and chase the only joy I've known since they locked me here.

Funny—when my children sent me to this hospital, they thought my days were over. They never imagined I'd meet you.

But you left anyway.

Days drag. The pills meant to "help" only deepen my despair. My children won't visit. They can't face the father who's "gone mad."

Shot of Chaos

The doctors know it's a dead end. The drugs that dulled my pain fueled my delusions.

Now, they have no choice. They'll stop the medication.

I'm not as crazy as they say. I know what this means.

Without the drugs, the tumor will devour me. The pain will return.

But so will the hallucinations.

And so will you.

I'll wait with a smile. This time, when you leave, I'll follow.

Roberto Brecht

The Pursuit

My life ends the moment he catches me.

That truth is the only thing keeping me moving. I've been running longer than I can measure. My legs buckle, my lungs burn. But I can't stop.

Worse, there's the darkness—an all-consuming void hiding everything around me. I rely on instinct and the faint trail of footprints guiding my path.

I know those same footprints lead my pursuer straight to me. Hiding is impossible. My only choice is to outrun him.

Yet no matter how fast I push, his guttural roars remind me he's closing in, his bloodlust rivaling my will to survive.

A new pain flares. Blood drips from my arm—a gash from some unseen obstacle during my flight. Adrenaline had masked it until now.

This makes me wonder: Why am I running? I don't know where I am, who's chasing me, or why. Only instinct drives me. That, and the terror of his footsteps pounding closer.

Shot of Chaos

Too late to stop. My body crumbles. My heartbeat thunders in my skull. I can't last much longer.

He's right behind me. I feel his hand graze my neck—then the darkness betrays me first.

I plunge into an endless pit. As I fall, I look up and see my pursuer.

A bloodied mirror of myself stares back, ragged and snarling, screaming from the edge of the abyss.

My body slams into the ground. Miraculously, I'm alive. The pit's floor is dim, but not enough to hide the figure scrambling away—my own back, fleeing.

I have to save myself. With a desperate scream, I chase after me.

Roberto Brecht

War

None of us imagined life could change so suddenly.

When the TV announced we were at war, half the country cheered; the other half mourned. Yet no one, on either side, understood how we'd reached this point.

That night, silence smothered the nation. The last war had ended generations before we were born. We had no idea what to expect.

The next morning, nothing changed—except the war became our only topic. We debated it, fought over it, yet life carried on.

Occasionally, we'd hear of a distant relative drafted, but weeks passed with little impact. The war felt too remote to matter.

We had bigger problems: bills to pay, bread to put on the table.

Then, on an ordinary afternoon—long after the war had faded from minds—we felt its first true blow. The city fell silent, just like the night of the announcement. People froze, tense, as if sensing what came next.

Shot of Chaos

The air thickened. A chill crawled down spines. Eyes met, heavy with unspoken dread.

Seconds before the first blast, dogs howled in warning.

A few recognized the danger, but it was too late. The first bomb fell. Dozens died.

More bombs followed. Dozens became hundreds, then thousands.

The buildings and homes we'd known all our lives vanished. Debts and promotions meant nothing now. Survivors, who'd once treated war as ideological debate, stood amid ruins.

The city's chaos gave way to survivors' sobs and the dead's silence.

That night, the country awoke. The war had finally arrived—and with it, a collective thirst for vengeance and forced unity.

In a hidden bunker, generals congratulated the president. At last, a leader willing to bomb his own nation to unite his people.

Roberto Brecht

Awakening

"I don't know what's more terrifying about waking up after so many years: the loneliness, or the disbelief at what I see.

Yes, you might have read about me. My awakening was hailed as a miracle nationwide, and my sudden disappearance a mystery. But what would you do if you woke from a years-long coma, surrounded by strangers probing your life, yet utterly alone?

I fled to a sprawling city where no one knew me. Surrounded by crowds, I became invisible—a relief after the spotlight. But what I thought was invisibility soon revealed itself as something worse. When I dared to rejoin the world, I was met with venomous indifference. It made no sense—until I realized it was about my skin tone. The future had resurrected a forgotten apartheid, barring me from spaces deemed unfit for my race.

Back then, I still clung to words like 'rights' and 'hope.'

Days passed, and I learned survival meant silence. Opinions could still be voiced, but dissent brought retaliation. Conform or be crushed.

Shot of Chaos

Bible-carrying men patrolled everywhere. If not physically holding scripture, it was etched into their minds. These self-appointed judges policed morality, punishing any deviation. The future felt medieval— guns replacing torches, God and country above all.

Their 'interpretation' even justified punishing me for walking alone at night. When I sought help, they asked why I hadn't 'said no.' How do you refuse a man with a holstered gun and God on his lips?

The system I once trusted offered no refuge. Resistance groups were branded terrorists, silenced to fuel the nation's perpetual war.

I was lonelier than when I first awoke. Silenced. Violated in body and soul. Desperate to escape this new world.

Then, this morning, a gunshot—louder, closer—jolted me awake.

I followed the sound and found a body. A young man in flamboyant clothes—unseen in this era—lay dead, a bullet hole in his forehead. Another 'terrorist' eradicated. No one approached. No one cared.

Sunlight glinted off the metal at his waist: a gun.

I took it. Not for power, but disgust—joining their game.

Holding it, I remembered waking in that hospital months ago, hailed as a miracle. Now I see it as punishment. Miracles don't exist. I was revived only to suffer.

With this weight in my hands, I wish I had the strength to fight. But it's too late.

So I pour my last energy into writing this farewell. May whoever finds it be stronger. Don't let them win.

Now, with my first smile since awakening, I press the gun to my temple—praying I won't wake up this time."

Metamorphosis

The tension was constant—any moment, he could transform.

It took years to understand what was happening. Until then, he'd only wake in random places with no memory of the night before.

Sometimes, his body bore strange marks. Other times, blood. Guilt-ridden, he'd rush home and cry for days, clueless why.

After a few transformations, he isolated himself. Moved cities. Stayed alone. Safer for everyone.

Alone, he built a fragile routine: work from home, grocery runs, cooking, TV, bed before dark. He didn't need friends. He needed control.

This held for years. But daily, the thirst grew. No matter his efforts, he couldn't live like this forever.

Sometimes it was a smell. Sometimes the night's allure. Each day, the craving worsened, the transformation inching closer.

Until he snapped. Years of isolation. He deserved this—one night to unleash his true self.

Roberto Brecht

He planned carefully. Didn't want to ruin his life. He traveled to a remote cabin where no one knew him.

Time to transform. After so long, he'd free the monster within.

All it took was a single drop.

The first sip burned. His brain swelled, eyes reddened. Aggression and rage flooded his veins. He roared in ecstasy.

Blackout.

Morning revealed the familiar scene: gashes, torn clothes, blood, a knife. A cold body beside him.

He was himself again. Ashamed, he fled the cabin, vowing: the monster must die.

He returned home, repentant. He'd never let another drop of alcohol touch his lips.

Black Flesh

Black flesh is the cheapest on the market.

I didn't know I was about to learn the lesson that would shatter my life.

The past few days had been hell. Cops patrolled our favela daily, clashes constant. Tension thickened the air.

A normal day. I woke up, turned on the TV, ignored the usual gunfire. Never imagined I'd never finish the cartoon I was watching.

A crash louder than bullets. Our door splintered open. A gunshot—deafening.

The cop's face twisted from hatred to shock. Desperation. Fear. Only when I looked down did I see my brother on the floor, his shirt blooming red.

I didn't scream. The cop didn't either. He just turned and left. Time froze.

My mother shattered the silence with a wail of agony. She cradled his body, screaming, "He's three! He's three!"

Everything felt unreal, like I was floating outside myself. When I finally moved, my mouth betrayed me: "The cop... he just... he..."

Roberto Brecht

The funeral was the next day. A sea of faces demanded justice. I couldn't stop talking. Couldn't stop shaking.

My brother was three. Three years old, killed by a cop too cowardly to face what he'd done. Too indifferent to care about another Black life.

Our protest grew. A news crew came. We showed them photos, his bloodstained shirt. We screamed into microphones.

The next day? A footnote among countless others. His name barely mentioned—just another "casualty" in the "war on crime."

Meanwhile, headlines glorified a white actress's new lipstick and a white couple's third reconciliation.

But the true lesson came from the photo printed above my brother's obituary.

There he was—the killer—smiling, honored for his "peacekeeping efforts" in the favela he'd terrorized.

The Gift

All families are unique, but the Ioroque family had a gift. They knew the exact day they would die.

Arthur remembered his first encounter with the Gift. He was with his family when his grandfather suddenly began to weep. Though strange, no one seemed shocked.

That day, his father also cried while explaining the curse they bore: every family member died at 75, always on May 14. It was May 13.

The next day, Arthur's grandfather went for a walk and never returned. His body was found days later.

Though grieving, Arthur embraced his "limited immortality," vowing to live recklessly until his appointed day.

He grew up fearless—skydiving, racing, surviving accidents that should've killed him. Every May 14, he celebrated another year cheated from death. This continued until his father's 75th birthday.

His father's death shattered him. Childless, Arthur was now the last of the Ioroques. The Gift would claim him in 25 years.

Roberto Brecht

Each passing year gnawed at him. He kept living on the edge, but inside, he unraveled.

Years. Months. Weeks. Until he turned 75, on the fateful May 13.

He gathered everyone he loved and mourned his own death in advance.

On May 14, he felt inexplicably healthy. Determined to spend his final hours alone, he wandered to a moonlit cliff—the most beautiful place he'd ever seen.

At 11:45 PM, he sat at the edge, closed his eyes, and welcomed the autumn wind. A perfect way to die.

But midnight came and went. He stared at his watch in disbelief. He should be dead.

Crushed, he realized the Gift was never real— just a lie passed through generations. But it was too late. After a lifetime preparing for this end, he couldn't go on.

He gazed at the moon one last time and, like every loroque before him, leapt into the void.

The Return

It was September 2, 2038, when the first of them returned. Spirit, ghost, shadow, apparition, soul… Despite countless labels, the name no longer matters. They are here with us.

The world froze that day. A failed heart surgery left the man's corpse on a hospital bed—and his translucent "soul" sitting beside it, staring blankly. People fainted. Atheist doctors became believers. Media swarmed the hospital, but before skepticism could spread, more reports emerged worldwide: souls lingering after death.

Scientists scrambled for answers, but no instrument could detect them. Cameras couldn't capture them; hands passed through them. Theories shifted from mass hallucination to theology, all inconclusive.

Half the world called it a curse, half a blessing. Suicides spiked. Not all who died returned, but when they did, one truth held: their presence tortured the living.

I never understood that—how a loved one's return could be a nightmare. Until my father died.

August 12, 2040. His decline had been slow, but his death still shattered me. Worse was seeing him afterward: his corpse on the bed, his ghost sitting beside it—translucent, gray, alive yet dead. A paradox of grief and joy.

I approached, tears streaming, smiling. His hollow gaze drifted from the horizon to me, piercing my soul. I tried to hug him. My arms passed through. Nothing. Just cold.

Days bled into weeks. I spent hours in his room. He'd stare until he sensed me, then lock eyes—no words, no expression. Just that unbearable void.

Over time, I visited less. Guilt ate me alive. My father was there, recognizing me, yet I couldn't bear to face him.

I tried. For months, I forced myself into that room, only to collapse afterward. Until I stopped.

Years passed. The door stayed shut. I stopped smiling. Sold the house? Impossible. So I abandoned it.

On my final day in the house, I gripped the doorknob. Ten years since his return. Seven since I'd last entered. I trembled, sweating, praying for a miracle—that he'd smile, vanish, grant me peace.

I opened the door.

Nothing had changed. He sat, staring blankly until he noticed me. Our eyes met. No smile. No goodbye. I fled, screaming.

Shot of Chaos

Thirty years later, I'm here—dying of cancer, certain I'll never see him again.

Then I closed my eyes. And knew it was over.

Until I opened them.

I was back in that cursed room, on the same decaying bed. I couldn't move, couldn't blink. Only my eyes obeyed, darting.

He was there. Staring. Always staring.

Days? Years? Time died here. Two ghosts, translucent, side by side. Him watching. Me avoiding.

Finally, I looked up.

Our eyes met. I thought we'd vanish, embrace, laugh. But nothing changed. No expression. No peace.

Now we sit, forever.

Eternally together.

Eternally apart.

Roberto Brecht

Thank You

She didn't know what was more despairing: being outside her body, or the shadow with hollow eyes standing beside her.

Still confused, she tried to run back into her body but passed through it like a ghost. She screamed, but the doctors remained focused. No one heard—except the shadow, silently watching.

Minutes later, the doctors stepped back. Defeated, they left the room, leaving only her, her body, and the shadow.

The shadow no longer scared her. Maybe it was her 11-year-old innocence, maybe a deeper wisdom. She understood. Screaming wouldn't help. She accepted.

Her life hadn't been easy, but despite the illness, she'd been happy. She'd been loved by the most incredible person: her father.

Together, they'd laughed and found true joy. Every day was perfect, even the days pain pinned her to bed. Even then, her father could make her smile.

Deep down, she knew he suffered. But he was so strong—smiling until the end, insisting they'd overcome this together.

Shot of Chaos

Remembering him, a pain she'd never felt before pierced where her heart should be. She collapsed, sobbing—not for herself, but for him.

The shadow waited.

Suddenly, she stood and met its gaze. Not with anger, not with sorrow. With hope.

The shadow understood. No words needed. Her final wish would be granted.

With a jolt, her father woke. Despite three sleepless nights, he couldn't believe he'd dozed off during her surgery.

He tried to recall his dream, but the memory faded.

All he wanted was to hold his daughter again. Then the door opened.

He didn't hear the doctor's words. His eyes locked on his daughter—now a flicker before him—whispering her last:

"Thank you."

Roberto Brecht

Testimony

After years of suffering, she decided to speak her truth.

She'd seen him on TV countless times, no longer feeling rage or sorrow—just hours of numbness whenever he appeared. But this time was different.

This time, she saw the way he looked at the woman beside him. That was the final straw.

He'd gazed at her the same way years ago, back when she still admired and followed him. What followed that gaze was the deepest pain she'd ever endured.

Years of silence as he lived untouched by consequences.

But watching him now, she realized she'd never heal. She'd accepted that. What she couldn't accept was him doing to another what he'd done to her.

So she opened her laptop and her heart, laying bare every hidden horror.

The first comments rolled in. Love. Kindness. Support.

Shot of Chaos

Shares. Thousands of shares.

More comments. More shares.

Her phone rang. She spoke. She wouldn't stop speaking.

Interviews. She was on TV. Exposing everything.

He responded.

Liar. Attention-seeker. Slut. Whore.

She expected it.

Liar.

There was love, but louder, there was hate.

Her phone buzzed endlessly. Threats.

She stopped answering calls. Stopped leaving home. Stopped speaking.

After all these years, fear returned—stronger, sharper.

The love couldn't outweigh the pain. She felt powerless against the storm.

On the brink of surrender, she turned on the TV one last time, bracing for his denials.

But it wasn't him onscreen. It was the woman from days before—now speaking of his atrocities against her and others.

Roberto Brecht

She stared, breathless. Then quietly turned off the TV, laid her head on the pillow, and slept peacefully for the first time in years.

He'd never lay a hand on anyone again.

The Accusation

After years of peace, his secret was finally exposed.

He was asleep when the bomb dropped. Moments later, his advisor called at dawn, saying someone had fabricated a story about him online.

He assured her it was fine and hung up. People had always talked about him. Just another attention-seeker.

Yet he couldn't sleep. He grabbed his phone and searched for the post.

Few likes, few comments—but there it was. Cold sweat dripped. Why was she doing this after all these years? Gold-digger! How dare she revive these lies?

She'd pay. But not yet. Let the dust settle. No one would believe her. No one.

By morning, his phone blew up. Everyone wanted his side. He stayed silent, seething. She had no idea what was coming.

Then she appeared on TV.

No. Now he had to respond.

Roberto Brecht

He posted his denial. people knew him. He'd never do this. God was on his side. He didn't even know her. She was insane.

The nation rallied. Support flooded in.

The woman vanished. Silent.

He'd won.

Until the second one came forward.

Then the third. The fourth. The fifth…

All of them. All the women he'd used wanted a piece of his money, his fame.

Overnight, the truth exploded. Testimonies, videos, photos. Tears and pain laid bare who he truly was.

His power—built over decades—crumbled. His family left. Followers disappeared.

Alone, he finally tasted the suffering he'd inflicted for so long.

In that moment, he realized he wasn't strong. Unlike the women who'd endured his cruelty for years, he gave up.

A single gunshot to the head ended it. His suicide note? The victims' own words, reposted across his social media.

The Old Man

Despite another sweltering day—the kind that made sleep impossible, drenched in sweat—he had no will to rise. Getting out of bed these past months drained him completely.

This was the first time he'd left it in three days. But now, he had no choice.

He couldn't pinpoint when it began. One day, he just noticed he was alone and sinking deeper into sadness, until even leaving the house demanded energy he couldn't spare.

So he lived. Lonely. No family, no friends. Forgotten by all, his only companions the walls of his home and the bed that trapped him.

But today, he had to rise. An old promise bound him. Years ago, he'd been saved by this ritual, and every year since, he repaid that debt.

Age had weakened his body, yet it also made him perfect to step into the role of the one figure who'd ever given him hope.

Memories of past years surfaced. The sadness always lingered, but for these few days, it would melt into radiant joy—fueling him to endure another year.

Roberto Brecht

All he had to do was reach the door.

But first, he had to stand. Slowly, with more effort than he'd mustered all year, he pushed himself up. He rose not for himself, but for them.

The moment his feet touched the floor, energy surged through him like a jolt.

He had to leave now, or he'd never escape.

He dressed, adjusted the red hat, smoothed his long white beard, and stepped outside with his first genuine smile in months.

COVID

He wouldn't let an invented disease strip him of his right to come and go as he pleased.

When rumors of this "Chinese virus" first surfaced, he suspected communist involvement. Soon, suspicion became certainty.

Not his problem, though. The hoax was overseas. Even when it reached Europe, he shrugged.

Then the virus "arrived" in Brazil—right after Carnival. Convenient.

Next came the leftist rhetoric demanding everyone stay home. Absurd! Who did they think they were? The "woke mob" couldn't accept defeat, so they'd cripple the country!

He wouldn't fall for the COVID lie. He knew the truth—empty coffins, deaths blamed on the virus for political gain, fake numbers.

Even when his daughters begged him to mask up and stay indoors, he refused. He was a patriot, a law-abiding citizen, not some masked bandit.

Then the dry cough hit. But nothing would stop him from joining the pro-country rally. Just a "little flu"—worth enduring for his nation.

Roberto Brecht

That night, coughing kept him awake. Historic day, though! A crowd united by love for Brazil. He'd pushed himself, but it was worth it.

Fever. Pain. Struggling to breathe.

He woke in a hospital. SUS public hospital gowns! Garbage. He tried to rise but collapsed. Blacked out again.

Fragments of conversation: "lung damage," "no ventilators," "COVID." Leftist liars! Commie frauds!

Days passed between life and death. They found him a ventilator.

When he regained consciousness, a letter awaited—his ex-wife's first contact in years.

She blamed him for bringing the virus home, killing their daughters. They'd been hospitalized after him… no ventilators left.

Tears came. Then rage.

This was the final straw. He wouldn't rest until he destroyed what killed his girls.

Communism.

Valley of Shadows

Though I walk through the valley of the shadow of death, I will fear no evil, for you are with me.

The landscape is desolate. The bodies falling around me terrify me, but no more than the people who watch their fall indifferently.

What I want most is to give up, turn back, and leave it all behind. But I have you—the one who gives me strength to keep going.

Even without looking, I feel the gazes following me. Cruel stares wishing for my end. Stares that wound without lifting a finger.

That's why you matter. When I feel alone, I know you're here, and that keeps me moving.

The darkness thickens as I trek through this shadowed valley. With each step, death and despair coil tighter around me. Without you, I'd have been lost long ago.

I remember who I was before I knew you. Back then, I thought I could walk this path alone. But I was weak, nearly surrendering to the shadows, becoming one of them—until you appeared. You and your light revealed the truth.

Roberto Brecht

I thank you for guiding me. For shielding me. For showing me those dark stares are envy for my freedom.

But more than that, you taught me I can walk this path alone, to the end. You taught me to shine, and now my light burns so bright the shadows dare not approach.

So I thank you again, my love. You're the man who inspires me, who made me a better man.

And hand in hand, we walk through the valley of the shadow of death.

I fear no evil, for you are with me.

Coffin

He awoke with a start. Though his eyes were open, he saw nothing but suffocating darkness. The space was cramped, reeking of damp wood and soil.

The last thing he remembered was his bed, his servants hovering around him—angry that he, not one of them, had caught the plague.

He was sure many were celebrating his downfall. Since youth, he'd known fear was the surest path to respect. So he'd honed cruelty rivaled only by his power—power he still clung to, even now, buried alive.

Any other man would despair. Not him. His icy resolve had carried him this far, and it wouldn't fail him now. His first act upon realizing he was in a coffin? Noticing the rope tied to his wrist, connected to the bell above ground. A bell that rarely signaled resurrection.

He also noted the fever and pain were gone. He'd been cured. Somehow.

His eyes gleamed in the dark. He'd return more powerful than ever. Not even death could stop him! He smiled, imagining the terror on his servants' and enemies' faces. He'd be the Lord of Life and Death. No one would dare defy him.

Time to return. He tugged the rope gently. Waited.

Minutes passed. Nothing. How dare they keep him waiting?

He yanked again. Anger simmered, but he still grinned, picturing the panic at the bell's toll.

Silence.

He wasn't used to waiting. Rage eclipsed his cold logic. He grabbed the rope with both hands and pulled hard.

The rope—meant to ring the bell—slithered down onto his chest.

In that moment, his heart froze. The darkness thickened. The coffin shrank. The stench of earth grew suffocating. The gleam in his eyes turned to terror.

Above ground, his servants slept soundly for the first time in years, deaf to the desperate screams of the Lord of Life and Death.

The Walk

I was already accustomed to pain, but this time was different.

My parents had known for a while but thought hiding the truth would soften the blow. As if silence could dull the weight of goodbye.

I was nearly home after a three-hour drive, yet I still didn't know how to face what awaited me.

How I drove alone for so long without screaming, I'll never understand. It felt like a failed anesthesia—numb to everything but the ache, paralyzed yet raw.

I tried not to remember, but memories flooded back unbidden. The two of us running together, curled up during adolescence. The good days, the hard days. But the tears wouldn't come. They pooled somewhere deep inside, stockpiled after months of exhaustion.

I didn't notice when I arrived. I sat in the car, frozen, until the first tear fell. I steadied myself. I had to do this.

The house was silent. No one in the living room. A few more seconds before the final farewell.

Roberto Brecht

They were in my bedroom—the room where we'd spent most of our lives. The door was open. I heard murmurs: "It'll be okay." They were waiting. I had to go in.

Every step felt heavier. Tears flowed freely now, a path they'd carved long ago. I didn't fight them.

I entered.

My heart clenched. Then I saw him.

We smiled automatically, like always. The first real smile in years.

There he was on my bed. As furry as ever, as joyful as ever, but sick—so sick.

It hurt. Deeper than anything I'd felt for myself.

My parents stood nearby. We exchanged a fleeting glance. We couldn't linger—if we did, we'd collapse. Even weak, he'd try to comfort us, like he always had.

So we held it together. Despite every past fight, in that moment, we were a family again.

He understood. He always did.

The man in white approached. It was time.

I whispered to him, my face pressed to his. Years apart, yet nothing had changed—except me.

Slowly, his tail stopped wagging. He fought to stay awake, but his eyes closed. My heart shattered.

Shot of Chaos

With his end, the last thread binding me to my parents snapped. There was no reason to stay. I left without crying, without trembling, carrying a new hollow ache that would linger briefly.

My parents were right. The pain would come regardless. No amount of preparation could armor this.

Some truths could wait. Unlike my illness, the news about it could stay buried a little longer. I'd bear it alone for the few months left.

Especially now, knowing that when my time comes, he'll be waiting on the other side—ready for another walk.

Roberto Brecht

Vampire

Is it possible to win a battle against your own nature?

For 479 years, I've never struggled with death. More than that—I reveled in it.

At first, it was about the blood, the thirst. Soon, I grew to savor the terrified stares, the futile escapes. It made me feel more alive than anything since my transformation.

Centuries of amusement followed. I'd count the hours until nightfall, eager to hunt.

But tonight was different.

The moment the sun set, I awoke to a peculiar scent. My instincts marked her as tonight's prey.

I crossed the city leisurely, finally glimpsing the small, aging woman who'd moved into a humble home.

Something about her hypnotized me. She seemed ordinary, yet that scent—there was something in it. I needed to wait.

2 AM. Silence cloaked the streets. She was alone.

Shot of Chaos

Effortlessly, I vaulted the fence and slipped through her unlocked window. So reckless. Had she known how her scent intoxicated me, she'd never have left it open.

She slept in a narrow bed, her frail body etched with the marks of a life of hardship.

Being near that intoxicating aroma was unbearable. My thirst had never been fiercer.

I knelt beside her, took her wrist, and made a tiny cut. A single drop of blood fell.

I caught it and brought it to my lips.

This woman. She was pure.

A life without malice. No sin, no stain.

Memories buried for centuries resurfaced. With them, empathy.

She shouldn't die.

Frozen, I stared at her fragile form, doubt devouring me. I had to act.

The next night, I couldn't hide my grin as I watched her body grow cold.

In hours, the purest soul to ever exist would awaken—hungry. And the world's greatest kindness wouldn't resist the taste of blood and death.

Roberto Brecht

About the Author

Roberto Brecht Roberto Brecht is not special.

To the outside world, he's just another face in the crowd. A Brazilian man who checked every box—born, studied, advertising degree, postgraduate credentials, corporate drone at a multinational.

Few know that behind this unremarkable shell lies a restless, chaotic mind. A mind that has spent nearly three decades delving into the depths of literature and the many faces of horror.

After decades of preparation, that mind has finally dared to fuse these twin obsessions—unleashing the demons that once festered within.

Roberto Brecht is not special. But the demons now set free… They might have something to say.

Made in the USA
Las Vegas, NV
09 April 2025

20748838R00080